CONTEN

Chapter One
To Whom or to What had
Chapter Two
Away from the scene of mysteries…
Chapter Three
Or they were both very good actors ?
Chapter Four
Another Reality – Sweet Dreams
Chapter Five
The Messages and A Show Down
Chapter Six
He was to be shot and thrown or dropped into
the ocean
dressed to sink to the bottom.
Chapter Seven
Getting some Answers
Chapter Eight
"My sweet love" he whispered in her ear.
It took Lucy's breath away.
Chapter Nine
A New Family Enterprise

BOOK II

Chapter One
To Whom or to What had Lucy been prey?

The slender sculptured silhouette of a young women could be distinguished as a vague form in the morning mist. The young woman had an athletic gait and was advancing at a quick and steady pace.

Abruptly, she skid to a halt and held her breath, shivers were running up and down her spine and she knew that she was being watched and followed by something or somebody. She gave a sudden jerk then swung into full gear as she bolted and ran for her life in the direction of an isolated café which was lit up a few yards away.

The door was locked so she violently shook it and shouted "let me in" as loud as she could. As she was rattling the door handle a young man appeared from the back kitchen and ran to open the door. "Lock it" she ordered him to do which he was doing in any case "and switch off the lights." The lights were switched off from a mysterious source, but Lucy hadn't paid attention to that at that point in time.

Lucy was out of breath, so she sat down to get her wits about her; then to think. To whom or to what had she been prey? She and the young man were sitting side by side and Lucy could hear and feel his steady breathing. There was no sign of fear in him. That alarmed her, so she raised her head to take a look at him and saw that he was blind. The man whistled and his guide-dog came obediently to his side to guard him and sat very close to his legs.

Lucy was speechless. Then realising that there could be a back door she whispered: "Is the back door locked?" She felt the nodding of his head in the dark then he whispered: "There are three of them on the other side of the road."

Who the devil are "them" she shouted internally to herself in silence which wracked her chest and made the young man smile? Lucy smiled back at him then her breathing settled; so, she could then think. She delved into her pocket to dig out her phone and discovered a message from her husband.

She glanced up and realized that the blind man was "watching" her. She noticed a tiny camera positioned as an earring on the lobe of his left ear. She asked him who he was, and he replied that he was Mark and that somebody was pointing a rifle at them through a hole in the wall over there. Lucy was astounded and feverishly turned her eyes to the hole where the two barrels of a rifle could be seen by those in the know. Wow she found herself whispering to him then turned back to the message from her husband, but before she could read it, Mark was shaking her shoulder and hastening to her to follow him. She put her phone back in her pocket and obeyed him. He was obviously in radio contact with somebody who had a bird's eye view of the situation. Once inside the back kitchen he said that they were going to shed a light on "them" and "us". With one blow of an axe he sliced the rope holding back the lever making the whole garden flood lit with multicoloured lights and music and they just had enough time to see three men taking to cover. The three men taking to cover had enough time to see who was in the back kitchen as well. Well done Mark on both scores!

Gabrielle, the unknown one in the corridor was not taking any chances she fired her rifle at them, hitting one in the knee. The other two dragged him to safety behind a tree.

Lucy turned to discovering the message from her husband when her phone rang before she could read it. She hesitated to answer the call as she didn't recognise the number. Mark felt her hesitation and put his hand on hers to prevent her from answering. The ringing stopped and Lucy's heart leaped into her mouth and she felt sick. She just said: "I'm thirsty."

Lucy's plight didn't fall on deaf ears and the unknown real one came forth with a glass of water from a bottle from the fridge, no label, no stopper just a plain bottle. Lucy had watched her pouring out the water into a glass which was already on the table. Lucy suddenly didn't feel thirsty any longer and refused the glass. Mark, feeling her mistrust gulped down the water himself. Lucy felt stupid and even ridiculous but, she couldn't imagine apologising for her suspicious mind. As she had had time to think she wanted to know who they really were and what was in that message from her husband? But, just at that very moment, Mark crumpled up into a heap on the floor, out cold to the world (his left ear was facing upwards she noticed). Lucy had watched his crumpling up in absolute horror then her attention went straight over to the unknown real one who was once again pointing her rifle at Lucy's head and motioning to her to drink the second glass of water which she had just poured out for her.

Lucy didn't wait to be asked a second time she grasped the glass and threw the contents into the unknown real one's eyes (Lucy heard a slight sizzle as the water caused a short circuit in her headset). the unknown real one staggered backwards probably thinking that the water contained some harmful chemical no doubt, and in the midst of panic pulled the trigger on her rifle and blew a table leg to smithereens. Lucy grabbed the rifle and was just about to blow this anti-angel's belly to smithereens when she refrained, spun round and blew the door lock to smithereens instead then ran outside into the breaking daylight right into the arms of a very, very handsome young man a bit like a James Bond. "Are you Mistress Lucy?" he asked and then he kissed her passionately on the lips. Lucy let herself with un-refrained pleasure be kissed before saying, "Yes, I'm Mrs Lucy."

Lucy gently disentangled herself from the arms of her James Bond then suggested that they call for an ambulance and the police. Patrick, that was his real name, informed Lucy that it had already been done.

In fact, they could hear the sirens, so Patrick suggested that they scatter. He would take Lucy home and the other two would go in the ambulance to the local hospital for treatment. She readily agreed. Once there she thought I'll read my husband's message. They could go on foot as it wasn't very far from her dogs' kennels where she had left them for the weekend.

"Just a minute I just want to see if Mark is ok and then we can wiz over to your place." Patrick left her standing there in wait, so she decided to take a look at that message, however, the sirens were getting too close for comfort, so she decided to set off in the direction of home and avoid embarrassing questions. Who was on whose side she couldn't fathom out at that point in time? But why didn't Mark want her to answer her phone?

Why was that arc-angel wearing a tight-fitting mask?

After a few steps she could hear swishing through the leaves in the trees and thought that it must be Patrick catching her up, so she slowed down her pace. "Mark's fine" it said then informed her that there was nothing in the water as Mark had changed the bottles before she arrived. "What!!!" she gasped. (Where was his Yorkshire accent?).

Lucy realized that that message was of upmost importance and that she had neglected it and that that phone call was also of paramount necessity and she hadn't answered it. Crickey what a mess! She decided to make amends for all that as soon as possible but, she wouldn't mention that kiss, that delicious kiss that she was, at that very moment, reliving in her mind and body with the same relish as in Chelsea when Robert kissed her when, in a state of shock, she gave herself entirely over to the exercise. She shook herself and pulled herself together for an instance. Then smiling at these enticing recollections of passionate love and passionate sexy kissing. Wow, it was great she concluded.

She wasn't aware at that point in time that the unknown real one had been reproduced as a very high technical sophisticated avatar sporting artificial intelligence AND volumetric video shaping, like a digital puppet, from an unknown source and of course, nothing to do with the deity incarnated to conquer Evil on Earth.

Chapter Two
Away from the scene of mysteries...

Patrick was walking very close to Lucy and she could feel his electric presence next to her she was also enjoying this closeness when she suddenly remembered that she didn't know this chap and from all accounts he could be a "baddy". But she discarded that thought as it seemed absurd to imagine that she had played into the hands of those who wanted... wanted what? She couldn't answer that question at that point in time! But the three foes had become three friends and Mark appeared to be on daddy's side (Lucy was not then sure that her father was involved in this), or at least a "goodie".

They were, in fact, heading for her house and that in itself, was a relief for Lucy, who had been abducted before and was very much on her guard not to let it happen again. She gave a side glance at Patrick and discovered that he was doing the same, that is watching her every move and her reactions. She stopped walking and turned towards him and looked him straight in the face: "Who are you" she asked? He pulled her towards him and passionately kissed her again and again whilst caressing her unhindered breasts and bare back through her tight fitted leather jacket which was quite weird AND yet pleasurable to say the least.

When Lucy opened her eyes – horror and disgust! It wasn't Patrick but the unknown unreal one that she had been kissing. Gabrielle the unreal unknown gave out a hideous laugh from a mouth of fangs and disappeared into thin air. Obviously manipulated by an unknown source, a very clever unknown source indeed! Lucy in spite of her immediate reaction was admirative of this unknown source. How could she have felt the kissing and caressing from a digital puppet? Fascinating!

Lucy had been bowled over by the shock and was sitting on the ground shaking with her mouth wide open, but she could feel the pounding of heavy booted footsteps coming from afar. She stayed sitting down waiting for her legs to stop dithering. It was Patrick running towards her with a gun in his hand. This brought Lucy back to her senses and out of her wondering, questioning daydreaming, so she drew her own gun from under her arm and hid it behind her back. Her other hand was exploring her neck to see if she had not been bitten by a vampire. There appeared to be neither hole nor blood in her neck, then she gave a sigh of relief and laughed at herself for imagining that far from technological idea of Dracula in the wilds!

But what was it that gave her so much pleasure and at the same time was exploring her vulnerability to be captured or even kidnapped? Who was the person behind this artificial intelligence of passionate wavelengths that took so much pleasure in indirect love making and was he, also, experiencing phantasmal delight?

Patrick had arrived at her level and was obviously shocked to find her on the ground. Lucy was no longer sure if it was really Patrick or not as this "unknown thing, this digital puppet" could change faces and bodies (as it was programmed to do) and if it wasn't him, her gun was of no use to her at all. She hid her panic and excitement and said: "oh! It's you Patrick" in a high-class manner.

Did you get the phone call? What were the instructions from base? What do we have to do?

Lucy suddenly remember the message and the phone call. She put her gun back into its holster and got her telephone out of her pocket. No batterie, shit!

Chapter Three
Or they were both very good actors ?

Lucy decided to go home and to try and get over the morning's happenings, but she still wasn't sure about Patrick and she could see that he was wondering what the problem might be.

They reached Lucy's beautiful house in vast grounds and went inside through an enormous bulletproof glass doorway. At least Lucy went inside as she had asked Patrick to wait outside. The door safely locked behind her she ran into the study to plug in her phone and at last get the message from Bayà, her beloved Bayà!

A sudden thought ran through her mind that neither a bulletproof glass door nor windows would hinder the unknown unreal one. Her blood went icy cold and she ran to the door to let Patrick in to help her if need be and mostly from herself and from that kissing that she found irresistible, enticing and pleasurable and was wishing that it could happen again soon.

He came in as invited and looked around at the beautiful wooden scenery that occupied the entrance hall then he glanced at Lucy and decided that she was one of the most beautiful girls he had ever encountered.

He was very much a man, even if Lucy was expecting him to change into the unknown unreal one at any

given moment; he was imaging
making love to her so very
sensually licking her whole body
and smothering her in kisses. Yet
he could feel her anxiety and so
could she, herself, as she was trying
with all her might to calm it down.

"What's the big deal Lucy or what's
up love?" Patrick, with a Yorkshire
accent, had decided to ask out
right?

"Well, you see Patrick" then Lucy
was going to blurt everything out
just like in Chelsea, but something
made her refrain then she just said:
"I want my husband to come
straight home now!" She then burst
into tears.

Patrick was touched by her attitude and decided to comfort her by saying that he was surely on his way there right then at that very moment in time (He knew, of course, that he was scheduled to land in 20 minutes' time).

"But what happened while you were waiting for me.?" "I was longer than I thought I would be because we couldn't find the person with the rifle. We had to give up in the end cos the sirens were getting closer and closer. Mark and his dog left at the very last minute with one of our men and went back to base." All these explications gave Lucy the idea that her father was at the bottom of all these happenings that morning. 'Base was indeed her father's office. She decided to think about that a little later as... (*Which phone call was Patrick talking about?*)

Lucy could feel the floor vibrating then hear the choppers of Bajà's helicopter landing on their private helipad. She sprang up with joy and ran to the back of the house and out through another huge armoured door. Patrick followed close behind and there he was so handsome, so beautiful so wonderful, so powerful and so very loveable. Bayà ran from the helicopter, he had to bend quite low because he was so tall (dark and handsome), to Lucy, picking her up and throwing her into the air then catching her in a wild passionate embrace (which pleased her no end). "My love, my one and only love!" (Lucy's teasing intuition was still finding that hard to believe but she pretended to at least).

Patrick understood at once that he was no substitute for her husband. He was her only love too. They were made one for the other in Heaven. (*Or they were both very good actors?*)

Bayà and Patrick saluted each other then Bayà shook Patrick's hand and thanked him for looking after his wife. Lucy watched on in pure, love and admiration of her husband. Lucy knew, however, without an ounce of a doubt, she had taken good care of herself and had enjoyed nearly every minute of it!

Come let's have a drink to celebrate our reunion and the success of our last mission. Lucy was dubious about the success of the last mission but perhaps they were not talking about the same mission she pondered or perhaps it was a phantasm, a dream, a nightmare she had experienced? She wasn't sure which, but she imagined that she would soon know.

They all went into the lounge and a servant brought in a bottle of champagne with "langue de chat" biscuits. Lucy gulped down the first glass of champagne and asked for more. She didn't know how she was going to relate the past happenings without talking about the kissing. Would she have deceived Bayà? No, no, no she couldn't have done that! However, she wasn't all that sure after all! Patrick was really a very attractive, tall, dark and handsome man too and so sensual and so sexy AND available it would seem. A real James Bond and quite irresistible! (She didn't know that Patrick was thinking how irresistible she was too and at that very same moment in spite of her husband's presence.)

"Well, my little darling, I think you have had a very hard day."
"Yes, indeed, very hard my love." (Lucy thought how stereotyped their conversations were becoming). "I believe you made the acquaintance of Mark, one of my best friends and a worthy member of our team. I saw everything that

happened to you through the camera in his ear."

Lucy was relieved not to have to relate all the events: "Did you see the unknown unreal or real one, the man I mean the woman or thing?"

"I did, indeed, and I saw her disappear into thin air before my very eyes, but I don't know where she went. Do you Lucy know where she went to?"

Lucy realized that Bayà had not seen everything.

Lucy went very pale and took another swig of her champagne before answering his last question. She began by: "Well, you see, Bayà, yes and no."

There was silence in the room and everybody's breathing could be heard a mile away as the atmosphere was so strained and tense.

Patrick spoke up: "We couldn't find her anywhere in the café nor in the surroundings, Sir." "I was late getting back to Lucy, Sir, and when I did, she was sitting on the ground in a state of sideration, I mean completely stunned out of her senses. She didn't get up straight away she seemed to be waiting for her legs to stop shaking."

Bayà turned towards his wife then asked her to explain in detail adding that it was very important. Lucy wondered why it was so important to him and how was he involved in all these happenings?

Well, I was hurrying home to recharge my phone to read your message darling that I'd been trying to find a moment to read all morning then I thought that Patrick had caught me up (strange, she thought, no sound or vibration footsteps just swishing in the air she remembered) but when I turned around to face him and greet him it was Gabrielle the unknown unreal one! She grabbed me into her arms and tried to kiss me! I was so shocked I pushed myself away from her grasp then fell on my bottom only to see her disappear into thin air after addressing me a hideous laugh! I think she must have sensed or heard footstep approaching to have departed so very rapidly. Or her commander-in-chief had decided that that was enough. (Lucy added enough "kissing" to herself).

"What an experience my sweetheart, come and sit beside me and give me your hands. My, they are still trembling my love."

Lucy knew that she was still trembling as she had been scared to death by the coming and going of Gabrielle, her code name for the unknown unreal one also of Bayà's discovering that she had (enjoyed) kissing another man. That kissing of Patrick could be forgotten she thought as she saw the upmost respect for Bayà in the attitude and eyes of Patrick. She was almost sure that he would never split or squeal on her. But the person behind the avatar had gone even further on the sensuality scale! Crickey it was fantastic! (But how did Bayà know where I was and that I was in danger? Did daddy tell him? Or had I told him that I was taking the dogs to the kennels for the weekend?)

"Who or what is this Gabrielle?" Patrick asked in awe. This brought Lucy out of her mental torture and she applied herself to the present moment.

"It would seem to be an organised kidnapping of beautiful women to populate or to people another planet in another galaxy. Unidentified drones have been sighted and signalled in the area. You Lucy were and still are on their list. Apparently, the captain in charge of the artificial intelligence operations from afar has fallen in love with you and won't give up until he has you for his mating partner. He has given himself an impossible task, indeed, "mission impossible" as, although I am very flattered that he finds my wife one of the most beautiful women in the world, I don't think he realises that I will never let her go and that's that. However, it could be and very likely is fake news, you know!" (*Strange, this coincidence of two kidnappings of Lucy he was thinking! Mine and an unknown source. Very strange!*)

Patrick was thinking that Bayà had seriously fallen for the hoax of Stephan and François or he was acting again...

Lucy was terribly excited as she couldn't forget the pleasure with Gabrielle as she had already experienced these extra-ordinary sensual avatars and their tactics. She just glared at her husband in sheer stupefaction. She would never squeal on "them".

Bayà wasn't losing any time he sent for his manservant then asked him to put on all the lights in the house and grounds. Next make a log fire for the evening "then bring us some salmon sandwiches and another bottle of champagne please John at the double."

John left the room to execute his master's orders and, as quickly as possible; so as to have enough time to phone to base and bring them up to date.

"I've been reading up on these effigies of extra-ordinary technological avatars Lucy and this is what I have discovered."

"You might both be asking why all these lights then I am going to explain.
These effigies can only be seen by us when they are in broad daylight or in bright sunshine. In fact, they get their energy, solar energy, from these sources so that they disappear from our sight deprived of them but that doesn't mean that

they are no longer there. Mark, for instance, can sense them but he can't see them." *Figment of the author's imagination so not based on scientific facts

Lucy let out a scream and hid her face in her hands. "It's horrifying" she said but was thinking how absolutely exciting and fascinating! She had always been interested in artificial intelligence and now was the time to explore it live. She didn't feel in imminent danger at all and couldn't wait to get started on intimately exploring it again.

"I also read Lucy that the only arm that we humans possess to eliminate them is through using laser weapons. *The laser beam lance enables pinpointing the targets and the quick triggers destroys them or their commands or control centres as well as their link with their satellite base in outer space. They have to be shot in the dark and the shooter has to wear a mask to protect himself from the laser fallout and backwash getting into his eyes." "They also

*Figment of the author's imagination so not based on scientific facts

have to be shot in a very precise spot in the centre of their foreheads where all their commands and connections are in place and fuelled by solar energy."

*Figment of the author's imagination so not based on scientific facts

Patrick was thinking that Bayà was really taking the hoax

seriously or he was exploiting it to cover up for his own kidnapping...

Lucy thought about how she had refrained from shooting the unknown one. Had she detected instinctively an Avatar or some very exciting new technology like volumetric videos or had she given her the benefit of the doubt of being on her side. He or she seemed so very real at that point in time and it could have been interpreted as murder. But how did he/ she get away so quickly? He/she must have been part of the team...but whose team she was asking herself. *I'm sure she got away with Mark and the others before Patrick got back to them.*

Lucy realised that her mouth was wide open, and she was hoping that she hadn't been thinking aloud, as she was so amazed. How was she going to deal with this? "Daddy taught me to shoot a gun but not to use a laser lance!" (And do I really want to destroy them; they are so very nice?) The kissing was haunting and fuelling her guilty conscious!

"We have no choice Lucy and you are going to learn how to shoot with a laser lance and how to pinpoint the centre of the forehead in a state of stress and shock AND at top speed."

Lucy just nodded and fell asleep with too much champagne in her belly.

Patrick was thinking that it would be paradise to sleep beside her... and caress her to sleep!

While Lucy was sleeping Bayà gave Patrick the rundown on the tactics to eliminate the Avatars, and instructions for the next 3 hours.

Patrick was to go and get Mark and his dog from base then contact the two others to find out if they were still able-bodied men or not then everybody back here within 3 hours. He could take Bayà's car and help himself to a mask and a laser lance from the chest by the side of the table over there.

Patrick was going to base as ordered by Bayà but, also,

unknown to everybody, to get his further orders from Stephan and François. He prided himself on his good acting and his trustworthiness towards Stephan and François. But could he leave Lucy alone with him? *This question was driving him mad!* He decided to leave but not before writing his phone number in the palm of the hand of Lucy while she slept and as quickly as he could while Bayà was out of the room in his office.

Bayà was also very tired so he went and cuddled up to Lucy, but he didn't fall asleep, he stayed wide awake and started reading the instructions for use on the laser lance and mask.

Chapter Four
Another Reality – Sweet Dreams

Meanwhile, Lucy was dreaming that she was floating in outer space in a state of weightlessness coming from nowhere and going nowhere till a spaceship came in sight. It cut out its engines
and a ladder fell down to welcome Lucy on board. She just managed to clasp it as she was floating by. She climbed the ladder just using her hands to guide herself upwards and into the spaceship. There was a round of applause as they explained that they had at last found her. She was very surprised that they had been looking for her. Then the ladder was drawn up and locked. Lucy was captured, a captive and captivated.

A beautiful being came from the back of the group in a long gold and silver robe, with very long golden locks down to his waist where a brilliant sabre adorned his being in a holster studded with diamonds and rubies. He took a very low sweeping bow towards Lucy and welcomed her to his realm. Lucy was wishing she had dressed for the occasion as she was in her jeans and tee-shirt again. Nevertheless, she remembered her manners and applied them to this high dignity. She was just about to fall fatally in love with this beautiful alien when she began to feel something or somebody shaking her. She tore herself away, with all her strength, from this state of beatitude to see Bayà shaking her shoulder. She awoke gradually and in complete peace like coming out of a shamanic trance.

"Patrick's back with Mark and the dog as well as the two others. Your mummy and daddy and the twins have arrived *surprisingly* too with their team and you know full well who and how many that means."

Lucy jumped up with delight and ran to greet all of them in one go. Lucy stayed a little longer in her father's embrace and he could feel that there was something wrong from the beat of her heart and her breathing. She smiled up at him and he said that they would talk later after breakfast. Lucy was happy with that.

John had lit the fire in the dining room, and it was splendid to have all her family and close friends around her for her Sunday breakfast. However, her dream kept haunting her from time to time and more especially that beautiful being kept coming to her mind and calling her name. She began to wonder if she had been bewitched as she was bewildered within herself and the calling was enticing her back into nothingness and weightlessness. For the moment she was resisting but for how long she didn't know.

She caught sight of Robert at the other end of the big oak table and decided to go around and sit beside him. Jasmine was not with him and her first question was: "Where is Jasmine?" "She's at home, she's expecting our first baby and didn't want to be involved in geopolitics any longer." Lucy was surprised by his reply and mumbled something like that she was sorry not to have the pleasure of seeing her again.

"I feel the same way, in fact, Lucy so I'm leaving after breakfast."

Lucy was stunned by the revelation that this mission could and would be the most dangerous and intense of all previous ones. The big difference being that she seemed to be the object of the exercise in a context of big business.

Lucy... the velvet voice called to her to come to him...

Robert saw Lucy falling into a trance and shook her to bring her out of it saying, "Hey Lucy came back here!" But Lucy didn't come back she had lost consciousness and had fallen onto the floor.

Her father had been watching her reactions all the while to what Robert was saying to her, as he no longer trusted Robert and couldn't identify the trance which didn't appear to be vodou so what was it? Was it shamanic?

He went over to revive his daughter and was alarmed by her state. She was in a state of beatitude!

Robert was sincerely troubled and didn't know what to do or to say. He turned towards her father and eventually voiced his opinion that her reaction was not directly related to what he had told her. Nevertheless, she had become aware of the dangerousness of this mission and because of her.

But it's not only because of her it's an invasion from extra-terrestrials to kidnap our girls to populate their planet or galaxy.

"Who is ever going to believe *that?"*
"It's too far-fetched! It's ridiculous!"
"To my mind it's Bayà who has introduced this fake news to cover up for the disappearance of Lucy after kidnapping *her.*"

"Oh! Really do you think so?" "Bayà kidnapping his *own* wife? Isn't that also far-fetched and ridiculous?"
Nevertheless, François was thinking that Robert was dead right!
"In every case, Lucy has fallen victim to psychological manipulation. We have to bring her out of it ! John bring a big basin of cold iced water please at the double."

John came rushing back with the basin and Lucy's father threw it on her face. It did the trick and Lucy woke up in a daze but back on Earth with her family and friends. Bayà was by her, nursing and rocking her in his arms to comfort her.

She didn't really need comforting as she looked perfectly happy.

Happy to be comforted by Bayà or happy to have been made love to by an alien, fueled by wonderful artificial volumetric intelligence videos implanted in her mind, she would never, ever, say that to anybody on Earth.

Lucy had asked him to leave her be on Earth but to allow her to visit him regularly as she could no longer bear the idea of a permanent separation. He was Love and she loved him with her soul and would join him forever in death. She decided to give a speech to the attendees at the Breakfast Party.

"I have a message for you all" she started then all eyes turned to her and their attention was captured for the rest of the news.

"I have a message for you all which is to say that there is no other reason for your being here this morning other than for having breakfast with me and my husband and that there is no new mission for anybody in the immediate future. So, we can all enjoy our meal and then go for a stroll in the grounds and park with Mark's dog then lunch together on the terrace as it is a marvelous day for that."
The whole room filled with cheers and happiness.

Robert said that he would be delighted to stay to lunch under the

circumstances.(*He didn't know yet that he had no choice!*)
Robert caught hold of Lucy's arm and discreetly asked her if he could have a word with her on the stroll in the park. Lucy agreed then went to finish her breakfast next to her husband.

Lucy recalled the supreme Love from that bewitching being from her dream and the beauty of his person and soul. He would constantly be within her and follow her every movement and thought she was sure and from time to time he would visit her in her thoughts, in her dreams and in quiet moments in the park and garden. They were ONE forever more. She wondered if she was going crazy or what but, for that moment, she felt that way?

Chapter Five
The Messages and A Show Down

Breakfast over, Lucy decided to go and have a shower and change into something pretty and feminine for the stroll in the park and lunch on the terrace.

The twins were playing with Mark's dog and Mark was playing too.
Patrick and the other young men were playing football and Lucy's mother, father and their team were strolling leisurely around the park. Bayà grabbed Lucy's father for a long talk on laser lances and Lucy could devote herself to Robert who really did want to talk to her.

Lucy strolled over to where Robert was sun-bathing on a low stone-built wall near the pond covered in pink waterlilies. Here I am Robert what did you want to talk to me about? The perfume from the pond filled Lucy's heart with spring delight and it brought back the kissing again to her mind and soul and how she would love to have a baby.

Robert looked suspiciously around to see if anybody was listening or watching them and then asked her why she had not answered his call.
"YOUR call, I didn't recognize your number Robert!"
"No, I was using another phone not to be traced."
"Why ever not?" (Lucy recalled Mark's hand on hers to stop her answering that call. *Whose side was Mark on?*).
"I sent you a message too and you didn't read it." Lucy was stunned and decided to look at the message from Robert as well as the one from her husband. She took out her phone from her pocket and scrolled

down to see her husband's message
first.

> *Don't go into the café*
> *Join the men following*
you
> *Go straight home*
> *Barricade yourself*
inside
> *I'm coming straight*
home

"You see he was having you
followed because he doesn't trust
you!"

"Personal (she remembered the
kissing) or professional?"

"Both."

"You're crazy; it's clear from his message that he was protecting me." ("But how did Bayà know where I was, and who was having me followed, she was asking herself? He didn't know that I was taking the dogs to the kennels to go and take part in a rally over the weekend with my friend Kathy and her husband, but I think my mum did?").

"No, he was paving the way to having you kidnapped."

"What did you say in your message, Robert?"
Lucy scrolled down all the messages and found one from Robert.

Don't go into the café

Don't speak to the men
following you
Turn tail and run back
I'm in the black car
Be quick
You're in danger

"You went into the café in spite of my message or even the one of your husband's and saved yourself in your own deadly devastating way."

"Just a minute, Robert, are you saying that Patrick, Mark and the others were in league to kidnap me?"

"No, they were playing a double game with your father who was aware of Bayà's plan. So, he, your father, intercepted all the filming and recordings sent from Mark's ear to Bayà to confuse him. What's more Patrick, Mark and the others are still here with us and faithful to your father, hence to you."

"I think I'm beginning to understand what is going on. There are two or maybe three different happenings."

"First, my trances and those are my business that I can't explain yet, but I soon will, I'm sure."

"Then there is the kidnapping and I think I understand why. I thought I was to be kidnapped for a ransom to get *something* very precious, some relic or other, but it's *somebody* very precious, that has been abducted and of course, before it becomes common knowledge, they want to get him or her back."

"I also believe that there are no extra-terrestrials but very high, sophisticated technological artificial intelligent avatars in volumetric videos in other words digital puppets being used to intimidate us all and create havoc like a cat among the pigeons."

Robert asked her if she had voiced this hypothesis to anybody else?

Lucy was surprised by his question and suddenly asked herself if that black car was the car of a kidnapper and that that kidnapper was Robert. And why did Mark stop her, on orders from **the master**

mind, answering the phone? Was Robert a traitor?

"But he is neither a kidnapper nor a man looking for fame nor with honour to defend. He's a nobody and a has-been for that matter; but these types of people with inferiority complexes can be very lethal in taking revenge so I should be wary even of Robert as perhaps he'd do anything for money!"

"Hey, Robert do you see what I see over there in the sun beams streaming between those oak trees?"
"Yes, indeed, I do! What should we do?"
"Nothing! Wait, I'm dealing with this."

Lucy got eye contact with Gabrielle and stood up to face him and his warriors

She acknowledged their presence and bowed to his **Master Mind** who confirmed his technological presence and prowess through a Morse code message flashed from Gabrielle's eyes...

> *I'll be back in your dreams* my love...

She then saluted the group recognizing them as warriors and not just a group of renegades.

Gabrielle saluted Lucy and swished away into thin air with his warriors.

It was thrilling to Lucy she loved technology and artificial intelligence like women in the ninetieth century who loved horse riding and driving cars! It was so exciting and sexy.

Robert was speechless.

But Lucy's father appeared looking for her. "What are you getting up to you two you look so serious?"

"Well, daddy, you see we've been thinking about the recent happenings and we've come to the conclusion that there are no extra-terrestrials in fact."

"Oh! And what have you put in their place my sweet little-one?"

"We, well I believe there are very high, sophisticated technological artificial intelligent avatars in volumetric videos and/or remote-controlled droid commandos. In other words, digital puppets at large but for what reason it is difficult to say at the moment and I don't know who is sending them to enact pressure on us all." (Or did she?)

"That's very interesting we could call a meeting after lunch to talk about all this and put in place a plan. What do you think?"

"I think it's a good idea, but I'd like to ask you a question first daddy, may I?"

"Fire away I'm listening!"

"Is Bayà a traitor?"

François was taken aback by the frankness of her question, but he answered that he was indeed a traitor and that she was in danger of being kidnapped by him.

"Why? Why is he trying to kidnap me I don't understand?"

"Because his sister, a reporter, has been captured by some rebel groups and they want a lot of money to give her back."

"But why ransom me?"

"It's because you are very beautiful my little one and you can bring millions on the white slave market."

"But daddy how could Bayà do that to me? He loves me !"

"He hopes to rescue you before they take you away and that is why you are coming with mummy and the twins to our place to keep you safe my little loved one and out of harm's way. You're not staying here one more night alone. And by the way Bayà is looking for you young lady and feeling very neglected. I think he's leaving again straight after lunch. I advise you not to mention anything I have spoken about just now. Pretend to be yourself."

Robert was looking very worried and he had sensed that the game was up. He was anxious to phone Jasmine to warn her that he was not sure of returning home as he was afraid of being summoned to court for treason.

Lucy was so taken aback that she forgot to speak about the Avatar Warriors or droid commandos She just nodded her head and followed her daddy to the lunch table on the terrace where Bayà was waiting for her to dine next to him. He looked so much in love with her that it seemed impossible that he was in league in such a risky action that might lose her forever alive or dead for that matter. He smiled at her and she pretended, as her father had told her to do, to be herself. Lucy smiled back and began eating. She looked up for a second to see a young man on the right-hand side of her father. She got a funny feeling of "déjà-vu" as she contemplated this very handsome man. Then, a sudden thought struck her – he resembles daddy as a young man. Goodness me he could be his son!

Lucy couldn't take her eyes off him and he in turn couldn't take his eyes off her. Then at one point in time their eyes met and they both burst out laughing.

Bayà wanted to know why Lucy was laughing so heartily and she told him that she was wondering who the man was at the side of her father.

"Oh! He's our new boss, he's taking over from your father who is retiring."

Just at that moment François stood up and addressed the table. He announced his retirement and that his wife and himself were leaving for an idyllic spot next to a beautiful lake in the mountains. He invited his associates to follow them as there were cottages on the grounds to be shared.

Lucy noticed that practically all his old team were very happy to leave and live with them in retirement. Lucy was glad about that.

Over coffee in the study, Lucy got to speak with her father.

"Daddy who is that charming young man who was sitting next to you at lunch?"

"My son."

"What?   Does   that   mean   my brother?"

"Yes, it does."

"Has he got the same mother?"

"No, he hasn't."

"Daddy, have you been living a double life?"

"Yes, my dear, I have."

"Wow! Does mummy know?"

"No, she doesn't."

"Who is his mother?"

"She is dead, she died in an avalanche soon after his birth. My double life has been bringing him up with love and affection. I loved his mother more than any other person in the whole wild world. He is to be your new boss and you will obey his every word."

"With pleasure." Lucy found herself saying, as she found him just irresistible and if he ordered her to kiss him, she would obey at once.

Lucy's father was reading her thoughts and he told her that it was forbidden.

François added that she was to keep her hands off him as he was her stepbrother!

Lucy responded vehemently that she wasn't promising anything!

"You're a cheeky rascal I order you to keep your hands off of Stephan."

"So that's his name!"

"Yes, after his mother, Stephanie."

"Does he have the same surname as me?"

"Yes, he does."

Lucy's father was somewhat amused by his daughter as he knew that she had always been in love with himself and a newer version of himself was a God send to her.

Lucy caught sight of Stephan advancing towards them and her heart game a leap to see him, to be close to him and feel his voice. At that moment in time nothing else mattered.

"Sir, he was saying may I have a word with your daughter."

François gave his permission but put Stephan on his guard against a temptress with no limits.

"Oh! Really! Hello Lucy…"

Lucy saluted Stephan and burst out laughing again.

Bayà was watching from afar and motioned to Lucy to join him.
He was leaving on mission. He wanted to say goodbye.

Lucy smiled at Stephan and told him that she would be right back and left to join her husband.

The choppers were already spinning and Bayà was dressed in military clothing. Lucy was determined to be herself and fell into his arms, looking up at him with devotion.

"I'm leaving, Lucy, I'm not sure to come back alive."

"Do you really have to go on such a mission my love? Stay here with me please I beg you my sweet love!

Let's make a family! Stay please stay with me! Don't leave me alone again!"

"My honor is at stake Lucy and I have to go." They were both weeping in each other's arms. Bayà drew away and ran and jumped into the helicopter. *That was the last that Lucy ever saw of her husband.*

Chapter Six
He was to be shot and thrown or
dropped into the ocean
dressed to sink to the bottom

Lucy was packing her bags when there was a knock on her bedroom door. Lucy drew her gun out of its holster from under her arm and said come in. She was aiming at the person who would come in and would not have hesitated to fire if necessary.

Stephan popped his head around the door and said: "Hi it's me."

"Your dad sent me to tell you that Mark and his dog, Patrick, his men and Robert are all still here and are leaving with us.as well as the oldies. He refused to let them go with Bayà and be involved in his personal story. Robert is fetching your dogs and the twins are ready. We're leaving with two helicopters and so everyone will be separated according to their affinities and so on."

Lucy carried on packing her case and wondering if she would ever see Bayà again and if not, what would become of her? She still had her family and friends and her dogs but no baby. No human souvenir as her father had had in Stephan. Nothing but memories of thrilling moments together. How she had loved him, but the fact that he was willing to ransom her for his sister had quenched her desire for him. She felt deceived, abused and abandoned and even more neglected than ever. It was true she had been in need of kisses when Patrick kissed her and even when the Avatar Warrior or droid commando kissed her! They were satisfying a lack of affection from Bayà and an urgent need of affection.

She fastened her case, flung her airman's jacket over her shoulder and went to see the others. Her dogs were there yelping to get to make a fuss of her. She made a beeline for them and life was beautiful again. Robert was there and anxious to speak to Lucy. He told Lucy outright that Bayà's so called sister was in fact his first wife and the love of his life and that if he managed to save her, he would never leave her again. That's why he told you that he was not sure of coming back alive as he would rather die with her than live without her.

Lucy was heartbroken and ashamed of not being up to the standards or worthy of Bayà's love. All these mocking up jobs and fake news to cover up for his deceitful behavior. All these hours, these days alone with rarely any news was because he was with her. How wretched she felt. She broke down and cried on her dogs' shoulders in total dismay.

Robert felt abject to have broken this news so abruptly to Lucy. He didn't know how to make amends or even how to ask for forgiveness for revealing that and for other grievous acts against her.

Stephan came on the scene and seeing Lucy in so much dismay and crying bitterly with her dogs he picked her up and carried her inside and placed her in her father's arms. The dogs followed and stayed to heel at her father's feet.

"There now my little one what has happened to make you feel so unhappy? Tell your daddy all about it." Lucy couldn't speak she just kept on sobbing. Stephan told their father that Robert had given her the news about Bajà and his other wife in an abrupt and heartless manner.

François didn't say anything he just kept on nursing his daughter in his arms and kissing her forehead. Lucy fell asleep and she was once again floating in outer space going nowhere and coming from nowhere. She could hear the voice calling her name and the spaceship came into sight. Lucy caught hold of the ladder and climbed on board. The beautiful alien gave a lowly bow to her and then took her into his arms saying welcome home then filling her body and soul with Love he comforted her. Lucy stopped sobbing and slept peacefully in her father's (and alien's) arms all evening and most of the night.

Her father was not sure that Bayà had abandoned his idea of

kidnapping his daughter, so he didn't want to let her out of his sight until he had got confirmation of his death. François had planned his death, in fact his execution, and was expecting the coded message directly that his orders had been delivered and fulfilled. He was to be shot and thrown or dropped into the ocean dressed to sink to the bottom. John came into the lounge with an envelope for François who opened it with Lucy still sleeping in his arms. The contents of the envelope were a coded message saying that the mission had been accomplished at 23H06 GMT over the Atlantic Ocean. François gave a sigh of relief and fell asleep as now there was no rush to fly home. He would inform his team at breakfast.

Chapter Seven
Getting some Answers

Peace and quiet was the atmosphere in the lounge where François and his daughter slept on and on …

Lucy was the first to wake and she shook her father to make him wake up too as it was one o'clock in the morning. François woke up gently and smiled at his daughter and said: "It's too early to get up my little one or too late to go to bed!" Lucy smiled back at him and laughed saying: "It's time to go to bed."

François decided to take the helicopters and to go home after breakfast the following morning and went directly to his bedroom where his wife Susanne was waiting for him. She was the first one to be informed. François could see the relief on her face, and she fell sweetly to sleep in his arms.

Lucy was wondering where Stephan was sleeping when a gentle voice said: "It's this way my sweet sister..." Lucy slipped into bed with him and fell directly into his arms and asleep in total bliss and security.

When Lucy finally awoke, she was alone in the bed and it seemed to be very late in the morning. She could hear chatting coming from the breakfast room so she decided to get up and have a coffee to start with but as usual she was starving and would soon follow on with eggs and mushrooms and so on...

Lucy glanced around the room and her eyes settled on Mark.
She went over and sat next to him and asked if she could have a word with him. He gladly accepted so she began.

"Tell me Mark what were you doing in that café? Were you expecting me? Then that person with the gun was it a real person? And why were there 3 men following me? And why did you stop me from answering my phone? Then again who were you in direct contact with?"

Mark smiled and motioned to his ear as he always had a camera on him, and he stroked his dog as his dog always had a microphone on him. So, Mark said nothing.

Lucy was stunned and dumbfounded by his silence and said nothing when she saw Stephan advancing towards them. Lucy felt a little bit embarrassed to have slept with him all night, but he continued coming closer and closer. Then he stopped in front of her and Mark. Mark immediately stood to attention and saluted him.

"Would you like to come outside with me please Lucy? It would seem that you are looking for answers again Lucy."

Mark continued saying nothing.

Lucy found herself a bit intimidated by Stephan's attitude and so she didn't say anything either.

"Well, do you want answers or not Lucy? Come outside!"

Both Lucy and Mark & Rover followed Stephan outside on to the terrace.

"Well, yes, I think I do, and the first question is who was Mark in radio contact with? However, I think that question has already been answered."

Stephan smiled and broke the ice. "Yes, it was me! In fact, I organized everything to prevent Bayà from kidnapping you."

"But what about Robert?"

"But Gabrielle the unknown unreal one who is her *master mind?*"

"One question at a time please Lucy!"

"Well, ok but Robert?"

"Robert is a traitor in league with Bayà for the money because he wants to give up working for a living and live in luxury."

"So, the black car he was offering was the kidnapping car?"

"Yes, and that's why Mark stopped you from answering his phone call."

Lucy suddenly felt sick and was afraid of vomiting all her breakfast. "This is disgusting don't you think so too Stephan."

"Absolutely, my sweet beauty!"

"Then the person with the rifle was taking care of Mark? So why did she fire at the men outside?"

"It was a put-up job. There were no injuries at all."

"But, the Avatars, Stephen who was in charge of them?"

"Yours truly sweetheart!"
"They were a hoax for Robert and Bayà. To make them believe that we believed that Avatars were trying to kidnap you and we needed

their help to stop them. They were really fooled by them. Robert was more dubious until he saw you communicating live with Gabrielle. It was at that moment that he realized that the game was up, then he tried to win you over by telling you the truth about Bayà. However, when Bayà left in a hurry Robert was held back by François. Robert knew that Bayà had left him holding the baby and that he would be arrested in due course."

Lucy felt humiliated and angry with Stephan for making a fool out of her and keeping her in the dark.

"But Lucy you were brilliant you didn't believe the story of the extra-terrestrials you fathomed out the technology which me and François were exploring for future missions. You were great and very analytical really! And you saved yourself showing extreme survival techniques, intelligence and ability."

"Yes, maybe, but I believed in Bayà and in Robert for that matter and they have both deceived me and put no value on my person as a woman, a wife or a friend."

"Yes, it's hard to accept but sometimes things and people are not what they seem to be. Some do for higher reasons and some do for the money.
Robert will be tried by an International Court of Law for treason.

I prefer you ask your father about Bayà."

"My intuition told me when I first met Bayà that he must already have a wife or two or three ! He was a very good actor but why did he want to marry *me*?"

"I prefer you ask your father, ok ?"

Lucy nearly jumped out of her skin when her phone starting ringing in her pocket. The name that popped up was "Jasmine". Lucy decided to answer and said: "Hello Jasmine" in a neutral fashion.

Stephan stepped aside as not to eaves drop on the conversation but just enough to still hear what was being said as Rover was still close to Lucy.

"Hello Lucy, I'm ringing about Robert I hope you don't mind?"
"Go ahead Jasmine I'm listening."
"This is not the first time Robert has committed treason over you!
The first time was in Chelsea when he refused to kill you to get the missing gem.
This time to try and save you from Bayà and an unknown source trying to kidnap you."
"The first time was noble treason, Jasmine.
The second case has to be proven and if it's the case his life will be spared.
Treason is not about my being abducted it's about losing your values and cheating your country

*and colleagues who risk their lives
every day for us all as guardians of
Love and Peace.*
*That I am the daughter of the
Founder and Commander-in-Chief
of this Organization makes no
difference at all from the moral
point of view."*
"So, you are refusing to help us?"
*"I have no say in the matter! It is
totally out of my hands!*
*If I am asked to testify, I will not
worsen his case.*
Goodbye Jasmine."
*Lucy hang up and put her phone
back in her pocket. Strange she
was thinking no message from
Bayà.*

Stephan came back and put his
arm around Lucy saying you said
and did the right professional

thing.   Lucy was completely overcome by grief, but she didn't cry she just walked away and went to see her father first, then her mother and the twins.

Stephan turned to Mark and asked if everything was going well for him and his dog?   Mark asked if he could have some leave to go home for a while? "Of course, Mark we'll drop you and Rover off from the helicopter, ok?   Get ready for parachuting! I'll ask for volunteers to jump with you."   Mark was happy with that and he phoned his girlfriend to say he was coming home on leave that very day. There was great glee coming from and around his phone and Rover was wagging his tail as he too was wanting to go home, and he loved parachuting!

Mark left to get himself and Rover ready for skydiving. They were both so happy they found it hard to contain it, but they knew that his best friend Tim was going to jump with them and take care of them both during and after the jump.

Stephan decided to go and get himself ready for the flight then go and chat with the oldies to wrack their brains for experience.

Lucy found her father on the helipad with his squadron and pilots.
She made a sign for him to come over and talk to her.

François excused himself and went directly to talk to Lucy.

"Good morning my sweet child."

"Daddy I want to talk to you Man to Man if I can?"

"Why yes, I think I can guess the subject."

Lucy was prepared for a show down and had decided to resign and look for a receptionist's job in Chelsea.

François, reading her mind again, said: "I'm not accepting your resignation my girl under any circumstances!" Then called for Stephan on his walkie-talkie to come and join them.

Lucy had decided not to cry but she could feel it bubbling up inside and it was difficult to control, however, she controlled it.

Her father, commander-in-chief, spoke first to explain his missions.

"I think it's the right moment to explain the coincidences of my mission and the aborted kidnapping of yourself by Bayà."

"I think so too daddy as I feel that I have been made a fool of."

"Not at all Lucy. You are mistaken my child. The person who has been made a fool of is Bayà and he has got what he deserved."

"What did he deserve?"

"He was executed last night and dropped into the Atlantic Ocean to sink to the very bottom."

"Just for wanting to kidnap *me*?"

"No, Lucy, he has been working as a spy in my organization and some of my men have been lost because of him and his treacherous manipulation and workings."

"Why did he want to marry me, daddy?"

"To be able to work from the inside and get all our faith put in him."

"I feel humiliated daddy! It's just too hard to bear at the moment."

"You're doing very well my sweet child. Not crying, braving the tide is all in a day's work you know in our Organization?"

"I thought he loved me!"

"I think he did in his way and he would have carried on having you as his wife had his real wife not been captive of some kidnappers herself."

"It's very strange but I also feel relieved that he is out of my life! He was hardly ever here, he refused to have a family, and we hardly ever made love! He showed never-dying love for me in public but in private he avoided me like the plague and left soon after landing and controlling things in his office that he locked up before leaving again and again. I was always hoping that he would stay and make a family with me, but he always left me alone."

"I'm not surprised Lucy. I'm so sorry that I didn't know this before. That marriage on the ship was by sheer manipulation, a masquerade on us all."

"Fortunately, we got the money back to the miners and they have done such wonderful things with it: school and teacher, medical center and doctor and nurse, shops and farms as well as electricity and sewage disposal and recycling systems. My word I'm proud of them and Tommy and Peter are going to university in the US this year to become international lawyers and experts in marketing and sales believe it or not!"

Lucy was proud of them too and in fact that's when she broke down and cried with love for them all! It was all so wonderful and worth the infernal relay get-away that took place to save them from the bandits' claws.

"So, my other mission was to try out this new technology which is absolutely tremendous my girl and you fathomed it out at such a great speed that I was so proud of you.

Ah! Here comes Stephan.

What's been keeping you my old chap?"

"Sorry for being so late sir, but I thought you two needed some time to talk and I had some things to finish off."

"Well, never mind. Glad you're here to give me some support."

Stephan looked from one to the other and then smiled and said: "It's all over now Lucy. Time to make a new start with your new boss and friend."

Lucy smiled and said: **"oh no** I'm going back to Chelsea to become a receptionist in a hotel."

"No, you are NOT" was heard coming from the voice with a

Yorkshire accent. "You are staying with me and the dogs."

Lucy turned around to see Patrick with her two dogs wearing parachutes and it made her laugh. The dogs ran up to Lucy and life was beautiful again. And especially beautiful in Patrick's arms while he was saying: "Will you marry me, Lucy?"

Lucy said: "**NO**, but you're so sexy and irresistible that I agree to be your mistress, the mother of your children as well as your best friend!"

"You're not bad yourself my lass! I'll make do with that for the moment and put it down to mourning."

All this was happening in front of Stephan and François who were so happy for her although Stephan said that he was sorry to be her boss and would have preferred to marry her himself and François said if he hadn't been her father, he would have married her years ago!

"I'm the luckiest man in the world I gather then because I've got the most beautiful and talented girl in the world as my mistress AND two dogs, a brother and a sister not to mention my devotion to my hopefully future parents in law and the team."

Lucy was thinking how she would have preferred to marry Stephan, as she was really in love with him but, she knew that nobody would agree to that. However, if he ordered her to kiss him or more, she would obey immediately.

Her father, reading her mind again, whispered "You little rascal you!"

"Daddy you are impossible! Stop reading my mind!" She whispered *back.*

Lucy knew that Stephan would stay in close contact with her as neither she nor he could resist the magnetic attraction of their love. It would remain a secret from everybody *excepting her daddy who had access to her mind.*
Stephan found a moment when everybody was looking elsewhere to wink at her and confirm the plan.

Lucy was happy with that and winked back.

First things first she told herself : make a baby (or two) with Patrick !

Her father said that that was a great idea concerning Patrick.

"OH! Daddy you're at it again!"

Lucy went back to thinking about one of the happenings which had not been uncovered and it was intriguing to know who was kissing her via Gabrielle and who would "see you in your dreams, my love"? There was also the velvet voice calling her name who was it? Why?

She needed answers again.

Chapter Eight
"My sweet love" he whispered in her ear.
It took Lucy's breath away.

She didn't see why she should go into mourning as she had been abused , deceived and neglected for years. She felt that she had been a good faithful wife in spite of this cold, unfruitful and unaffectionate relationship. She used to think it was her fault that Bayà didn't love her any longer, but she didn't know why. Now she knew why she felt better to be free again. Kissing was what she truly loved really! So, she went straight up to Patrick and gave him a long passionate kiss which he responded to instantly and gave her more love than she had had in a long time.

Out of the corner of her eye she could see Stephan suffering. She told herself that he would not be suffering for long as she was not going to deprive herself of this devastating love, she had for him. She would make her babies with Patrick they will be love babies as the love that Patrick had for her was just as devasting as the love that she had for Stephan. She would never get married again!

They all decided to go and get ready to be airborne and arrive in good time for supper in the mansion of her parents. Two helicopters were just enough for everybody, including John, the dogs and the team.

Tim came over to Stephan and informed him that he was volunteering to take care of Mark and his dog and to jump in tandem with him and Rover. "Please sir, may I stay a few days with him and his family please sir?"

Stephan was very touched and gave Tim leave for 3 weeks. Tim was dumbfounded and thanked him profusely. "Oh! Thank you, thank you sir thank you." Stephan just smiled back at him and told him to come back with Mark and Rover in three weeks' time.

Stephan then walked away to get his travelling bag and kit and get aboard the helicopter.

He was in the same one as François, Suzanne and the twins and Lucy. The old team was with them too and Patrick went with the others chaps in the other helicopter to organise the drop down of Tim, Mark and Rover over the farm amongst the cows in the middle of nowhere and report back to base in Chelsea. Patrick gave Lucy an enormous parting kiss and said he would be back with her the following week. «You are so lovely my sweet *mistress!*» They both laughed remembering the first words that Patrick, her James Bond, had ever spoken to her: "Are you *mistress* Lucy?"

Lucy looked around to find Robert and he was there in the same helicopter as herself. She felt relieved as she didn't want him executed and dropped into the ocean like somebody she once knew.

"Robert, she said come and sit by me please." Robert obeyed instantly and sat next to Lucy. Just after sitting down he burst into tears. Lucy waited for him to stop crying and then told him that she had decided to ask her father to drop the charges against him. "I can't promise anything, but I'll do my best Robert I promise you! I want Jasmin to have a husband and your baby to have a father. I love you all dearly." Robert was overwhelmed but managed to mutter or splutter that they both loved her too and were so sorry to have hurt her.

Lucy then got up and went and sat next to Stephan who discreetly held her hand in his trousers' pocket. "My sweet love" he whispered in her ear. It took Lucy's breath away. She suddenly felt exhausted and resting her head on Stephan shoulder, as she had done on the airman's shoulder in the Get-Away-Helicopter, she fell asleep to the droning of the chopper.

She immediately heard the velvet voice calling her name.
Then she was floating in outer space going nowhere and coming from nowhere. The spacecraft came into view and she caught and

climbed the ladder into this spacecraft of mystery.

The wonderful adorning figure took her into his arms and filling her heart and soul with love, comforted her so she could sleep soundly during the flight and wake refreshed.

Lucy suddenly woke up and realized that the helicopter had landed.

She disentangled herself from Stephan and stood up looked around and found that everybody had gone! She was alone with Stephan!

He stood up and grabbed her into his arms and kissed her as she had never been kissed before with so much love it was immeasurable!

He then said: "We have to go and join everybody for supper now!" Then he kissed her again and again saying "How I love you Lucy!" Lucy replied that she loved him too forever and forever!

"Do you know that nobody knows I'm François' son excepting you and me and François himself?" "That is the best news I've heard in my life!" "Let's go and eat I'm starving!" Stephan said: Ok but I'm raving to ravish you!" Lucy looked into his eyes and said how wonderful it was to be loved by him. He kissed her again and again then they went to find the others and eat.

The mansion was so lovely and the cottages around it were absolutely sweet and with every modern convenience as well. Most of them had three bedrooms and a little plot of ground in which to have a vegetable garden.

They were all busy choosing their cottages on the map when Stephan and Lucy came on the scene.

"Hello! You little lovebirds they all shouted!" Lucy was very surprised and so was Stephan but they both smiled and laughed so that no suspicion could be placed on their relationship. They went and sat away from each other and Lucy started chatting with her mother.

"Lucy, my little cherub, you were sleeping so soundly on your boss's shoulder that he dare not move! I hope you both haven't got a stiff neck!" Lucy laughed and replied that she felt completely refreshed as she had reached complete exhaustion during the weekend.

"I can well imagine, my love. I've heard from your father that you have a wonderful project with Patrick to have a baby n'est-ce pas?"

"Perhaps two or three if we are blessed!"

"How wonderful! Do you know that Cathy, your sister is expecting a baby?"

"Why, no I didn't how wonderful!"

"She met a young airman a year ago and they have been together ever since. His name is Tim."

"Oh! Golly is that Mark's best friend?"

"Yes, it is, and Cathy has already left to join them on the farm.
They all want to set up an organic farm with animal and fruit and vegetables. Making goat's cheese and honey, and so on...."

Lucy was absolutely envious of her sister and broke down and cried again.

"Whatever is the matter my darling?"

"I don't want to go on with these geopolitical missions maman!"

"But you don't have to my darling you can live with Patrick and bring up his children and he does the missions with the new boss Stephan."

Lucy suddenly realized that if she didn't go on with the missions, she would never see Stephan again. She also became aware of her passion for artificial intelligence that she wasn't sure to come into contact with as a receptionist in Chelsea.

Chapter Nine
A New Life Enterprise

"Mummy, do you know who the house I was living in with someone I once knew belongs to?"

"Yes, of course, darling, it's ours. It used to belong to my grandfather."

"Then I can make my new life from that house? Can I take it over? Can I have John with it?"

"Yes, of course, darling I was hoping you would."

"Then I can exploit the parklands and garden to my fancy?"

"I can grow organic flowers and fruits and vegetables and tend sheep and goats and open the parkland and gardens to the public? I can achieve wonderful things including giving a home to 3 or 4 immigrant families to live and work on the "farm"?"

"Yes, of course, my darling daughter. As for taking John, you'll have to ask him, and you'll have to ask Patrick if he wants to live there too."

"I'm going to ask him right now" and she ran down the corridor to the kitchen. John was busy with his boyfriend installing the new kitchen.

Lucy realized that John was her father's friend and would never leave him. She just said, "I've come to see your new kitchen John." John was beaming and told Lucy that he also had a new cottage and he could look after the vegetable gardens in the grounds with his boyfriend.

Lucy felt so very much alone.

She was wondering if Cathy and Tim and Mark and his girlfriend would like to live on the family farm? They could have houses built in the parklands for each couple. Tom could be the director with his training and organise survival courses in the parklands.

Lucy decided to phone Cathy.
"Hello Cathy, it's me Lucy speaking."
"Hello! Lucy, what a nice surprise."

With bated breath Lucy explained the situation and waited for Cathy to give her opinion.

"I'll call you back in 5 minutes Lucy I need to put the project to the others."

Five minutes seemed an eternity to Lucy who couldn't wait to know her fate for the immediate future and long-term family view.

The phone rang and it was her brother Tom.
Lucy answer immediately.

"Hi Lucy, the answer is YES! We'll all join you there after our 3 weeks' holiday needed to sell the cows and let the farm. We're all very excited and love you dearly."

Lucy was so very happy she ran to tell her parents their project and celebrate the reunion of their children.

François and Susanne were delighted and called for champagne all round to celebrate this good news.

John went to tell everybody to come and celebrate including Stephan.

Stephan heard the news and understood that Lucy was paving the way for their relationship to develop and at the same time make babies with Patrick. She was probably resigning from the Organisation, but not sure???? He knew her passion for artificial intelligence, the safeguarding of relics and the fight against injustice. So, he decided to wait and see and take part in the celebration. As not having the same mother the house and parklands didn't count in his heritage, but he would like to make it his home. He decided to explore the possibility of joining the group as well as running the Organisation.

John had brought into the dining room all the champagne glasses and biscuits and special Belgian chocolates for the occasion.

François asked John to celebrate too with his boyfriend their cottage and new modern kitchen in the mansion.
John was so happy to do so indeed he was.

Everybody who was to live in the cottages and grounds came up to celebrate.
Lucy looked around to see if Robert and Stephan had also come to celebrate her new life. Robert was still there and so was Stephan.

Lucy went straight up to her father and asked if it were possible to drop the charges on Robert? Her father replied that he had already done so. However, he can no longer work in our Organization. "Then he could come with his family to live in the parklands of our country house?" "Yes, of course, if you invite him to do so." "I'll ask the others."

Lucy then went to see Stephan to ask his opinion on her future plans for the country house and parklands and her family.
Stephan had a glass of champagne in each hand; one for him and one for her. He looked into her eyes and said, "Let's drink to the success of your plans my sweet entrepreneur! May I come too? I would like to make my home in that house if you allow me to that is?"

His request took Lucy's breath away and she couldn't speak. Stephan said that now it was he who was looking for answers!

She finally said that she thought that Tom would take over the study but there was a wing to the south side of the house which could be made into Base for him and even an apartment.

Stephan smiled and said that it was exactly the part of the house he was aiming at. "Then it's yours." she managed to say as she was laughing with glee she was stumbling over her words.

"In that way you can continue working for the Organization Lucy?"

"I'm not sure I want to, but I'm not saying no."

"Well, perhaps I can stop working for the Organization and devote myself to your project and creating an art gallery in the southern wing?"

Lucy couldn't believe her ears. A dream come true! She kissed him passionately in front of everybody and he responded with the same *insouciance* as they were leaving for a new life the following morning.

"Do you think you could help me elucidate the part of the happenings this weekend as far as my trances are concerned?"

She then came back to the live communication with Gabrielle and the message in Morse which was "I'll see you in your dreams again, my love!

Robert came over at that point in time to tell Lucy that Jasmin didn't want to go to the country house but would love to stay with her parents if they allow them to do so.

" I'm sure they will Robert, no doubt about that. she enthusiastically replied as Jasmin has always lived with them."

We were just mentioning the live contact with Gabrielle and the message in Morse which was : "I'll see you in your dreams again, my love"

"Who do you think it was Robert?"

Robert looked perplexed and said that he thought all that was over and done with.

"No, Robert it isn't at all."

Why not?

"Because I still have those dreams and trances and I want to get to the bottom of them, that's why!"

"I'm sorry Lucy but I've no idea. I know it wasn't Bayà nor the one in the café that's all I know."

"Ok thank you I'll tell you when I know."

Stephan had been listening to the conversation so he added that he thought that he was the only **master mind** behind this invasion, however, it would seem that there was another source and that source has its eye on you girl. I'm not saying that it's evil, but it seems to be operating through Love which can be used to gain power.

I think we both agree that they were real and so capable of physical actions like firing a rifle at us. However, their disappearing into thin air doesn't fit with that. "So, where do we go from here?"

"We go back to the second glass of champagne on the rocks." Lucy suggested and decided to go on celebrating the country house, organic farming and parklands project with everybody including the radio video link with the twins and their friends on the farm.

Perhaps, thought Lucy it **is** all over and done with... "But perhaps not!"

End of Book II

Printed in Great Britain
by Amazon